# Esmeralda

—— *and* ——

## the Night Creatures

—— *by* ——

## Heather Henning

Illustrated by Roger Best

Kevin Mayhew

First published in 1998 by
KEVIN MAYHEW LTD
Rattlesden
Bury St Edmunds
Suffolk IP30 0SZ

0 1 2 3 4 5 6 7 8 9

ISBN  1 84003 153 0
Catalogue No  1500169

Cover picture by Roger Best
Book design by Jaquetta Sergeant
Edited by David Gatward
Typesetting by Louise Selfe
Printed and bound in Belgium

# Contents

Pinecroft Farm

# Esmeralda

*and*

the Night Creatures

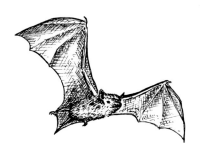

Flip, flip, flap, went Esmeralda's tiny wings.
'Adventure!' she squeaked, 'adventure!'

Flip, flip, flap, went Esmeralda's tiny wings. 'Adventure!' she squeaked, 'adventure!' All around her, snuggled up in a warm roost in the corner of the long barn were several hundred other baby Pipistrelle bats. Like babies everywhere, they wanted to play and have fun. Their grey-brown mothers brought them gnats and little moths to eat.

The young bats grew quickly and they were soon taking flying lessons round the barn.

'Look at us!' called Esmeralda, diving among the cobwebs with her friends and missing them by inches. The clicks from their special bat 'radar' helped to stop them crashing into one another in the dark.

Soon, very soon, they were ready to go outside for the first time. The mother bats led the excited babies out through the barn window.

'Remember to return to the roost before daylight,' squeaked Esmeralda's mother.

Esmeralda was tired after her first night's flying,
and clung to a tree in Bluebell Wood.

'Of course,' replied Esmeralda, but she soon forgot her promise as little ones sometimes do, in the fun of chasing her friends.

Now Farmer John Hayden's barn at Pinecroft Farm was home to other night creatures as well as bats. He and his son had built a huge stack of straw bales up to the roof, dividing the building in two. In the far end of the barn lived a pair of beautiful white barn owls. Their children, Misty, Minty and Mango, had just hatched from three round white eggs. The owls in the east end flew in and out of the barn's high east window, and the bats flew in and out of the west.

Esmeralda was tired after her first night's flying, and clung to a tree in Bluebell Wood which bordered the farm. She held on fast and fell asleep.

Finally she landed with a crash at the feet
of Minty, Misty and Mango.

When she awoke she was all alone. She was very frightened. 'A-l-o-n-e,' whimpered Esmeralda. She could see the sun rising through a low mist over the farm fields and remembered her mother's words: 'Return to the roost before daylight.'

'Help! I'm lost!' she thought, feeling very afraid. 'Where is everybody?'

All the other baby bats had returned safely to roost. The only sounds she could hear were the early morning sounds of the farm. The cows were being milked, and Farmer Hayden's wife Peta was calling the hens to breakfast.

As Esmeralda watched, she saw one of the big barn owls fly through the east window of the barn with food for the owlets. In her terror, she launched herself from the wood and followed.

But when she arrived in the barn, where was the roost? Where were the other bats? Where was her mother?

Esmeralda flew round and round the rafters, squeaking with fear. Finally she landed with a crash at the feet of Minty, Misty and Mango.

'I say, o-oo-ld thing, watch where you're go-oo-ing,' grumbled Minty.

'I nearly mistook you for a mou-oo-se,' said Misty.

'Mum! Mum!' shrieked Mango. She was an excitable young owl, and a little less clever than the other two.

Esmeralda picked herself up and stared at the huge white fluffy owlets. Pipistrelle bats are tiny, not much longer than your finger, so Minty, Misty and Mango looked like giants to her.

'Where am I?' she wailed. 'I can't find my way home. My mother told me not to go out in the daytime.'

'Well! You'd better stay with us,' said Ona the mother owl kindly, and she smiled at Esmeralda.

So began Esmeralda's life with the barn owls. She was very young and knew little about being a bat. The best plan seemed to be to copy Minty, Misty and Mango.

'Ooooops.' Her first attempt to eat a mouse had the owlets in fits of laughter. The mouse was bigger than she was! Baby owls swallow their food whole. Watching Esmeralda trying to open her tiny mouth wide enough for a whole mouse made Mango laugh so much that she got hiccups.

'I'd better bring you some beetles for supper,' sighed Ona, 'or you might cho-oo-ke.'

Once the day was over, Minty, Misty and Mango spent their time flapping and stretching their wings. The nest became very crowded. After being knocked out twice, Esmeralda crawled away along a wooden rafter. She hung there by her toes out of the way, looking like a rumpled umbrella. The owlets were amazed.

'Why don't you-oo fall off?' laughed Minty.

'Doesn't hanging upside dow-oo-n give you a headache?' asked Misty.

Mango started to walk out along the rafters copying Esmeralda, but Gregory the father owl rescued her just in time! 'Bats hang upside dow-oo-n to rest,' he boomed in his gruff voice, 'but owlets do not. You little ones will be flying soon enough!'

Two nights later, Misty took his first wobbly flight around the barn, helped by a delighted Esmeralda. Minty, who was nervous at first, soon joined him, but Mango had to be helped from the nest by her mother because she was too frightened to jump out on her own.

Esmeralda crawled gasping and spluttering across
the straw on the barn floor.

As they rested after a hard evening's flying, Esmeralda said to Misty, 'Why am I still so different from you? After all, we can both fly. Why do I have wings on my fingers and no feathers? And I'm such a dirty colour. I'd love to be white like you.'

Misty thought hard for a moment. 'Just before supper,' he said, 'I saw Farmer Hayden put something from a tin on the barn doors. When he had finished, the door was white like me. Perhaps that might help you look like us!'

So late that night when Ona and Gregory had gone hunting, Esmeralda and the three owlets flew down to the floor of the barn. The open tin stood by the barn doors. Esmeralda landed on the edge and fell in! She made a grab for the rim with her tiny thumbs and managed to haul herself out. Minty and Misty stared in horror.

Mango, who was the youngest and the silliest, set up a great fluttering and squawking. 'Wow, Esmeralda!' she yelped. 'You-oo did want to look like us, didn't you?'

Esmeralda crawled gasping and spluttering across the straw on the barn floor. She spat a blob of white paint from her tiny mouth. She was so sticky that she could hardly move. By now all three young owls were calling for their parents. They made such a noise that John stopped in the middle of his supper at the farmhouse.

'What a din!' he said to his wife. 'Coming from the barn, I'd say. I'd better take a look. Come, Biffy!'

Biffy the farm dog rose from the hearthrug and followed her master out of doors. They crossed the yard together to the big barn.

As soon as the owlets heard John lift the latch on the barn doors, they flew up to hide in the rafters. Esmeralda wanted to join them, but the white paint had clogged her wings. Biffy, nosing round the tin, found her at once.

'Woof, woof,' she barked.

John hurried over, and bent down to stare at the small sticky object that was Esmeralda. 'Hey-up, Biffy, what's this?' he said. 'Whatever it is, it's fallen in the paint. I'd better take it to the kitchen. Peta will clean it up before the paint dries hard.'

He wrapped Esmeralda in his handkerchief and carried her carefully back across the yard, Biffy trotting at his side. Peta filled the stone sink in the utility room with warm soapy water, and began to clean Esmeralda's fur.

'We'll need a warm place to dry it out,' Peta said. 'It's

had quite a fright, but it'll be all right, I think. Whoever heard of a white bat? That would look silly! Louis,' she called to her son, 'where's the old stone hot water bottle? Find it and fill it with warm water – not hot, mind! – and we'll keep the little bat in a shoebox by the range.'

'What beats me,' said John, 'is that it was in the east end of the barn where the owls live. Perhaps it got lost. When it's better, we must help it find its way home.'

Esmeralda lay on the towel on top of the hot water bottle in the shoebox, with her eyes shut. She felt too groggy to be frightened, and she was sure that her enormous rescuers meant her no harm.

Louis lifted Esmeralda up and threw her gently in the air.

Two days passed. At night she heard Minty, Misty and Mango calling on their hunting trips in the fields around Pinecroft Farm and she missed them.

On the evening of the third day Esmeralda felt well enough to climb out of the box. When Peta returned from feeding the hens, she found the small creature hanging from a curtain rail near the kitchen door.

'Look at that,' she said to Louis, who had just come in from his day's work. 'It's about time for the bats in the barn to be out and about. Shall we see if this little one wants to join them?'

They carried Esmeralda out into the twilight. Sure enough, several bats were swooping and diving around the west window. More emerged as they stood watching. Esmeralda wriggled and squeaked. John, who was walking across the yard, laughed when he saw the bat. 'Let it go, Louis,' he said. 'You won't hold it much longer.'

Louis lifted Esmeralda up and threw her gently in the air. She opened her wings and, fluttering happily, went straight to join her old friends.

'Click, click, hello!' they greeted her. 'Where have you been? We've missed you so much! Click, click, click, isn't this fun?' Esmeralda was so pleased to be back that she forgot to answer. She zigzagged joyfully across the starry sky.

Cuddling up to her mother in the roost early next morning, she understood why she was so different from Minty, Misty and Mango. She wasn't an undersized white owl, she was a full-sized, brown, furry, mouselike bat.

'Last night,' she thought, smiling to herself, 'I had a lovely meal of gnats and moths. Just think, I once tried to eat a mouse, *whole!*'

As for the tin of white paint, Esmeralda shuddered to think what might have happened if Farmer Hayden hadn't found her.

The long warm days of summer had now arrived. Life at Pinecroft Farm continued much as usual. There were cows to be milked and crops to be weeded. John and his family worked from dawn to dusk. They liked the wild creatures that lived on and around the farm and often stopped to watch them. But there was one family of animals that John did not like. Their favourite game was turning over the dustbins and eating the scraps left from the farm kitchen. If he or Louis spotted them after dusk, they usually frightened them away.

But this particular night, the whole family had gone to visit friends, and Biffy was shut up indoors. As Esmeralda took her usual evening flight, she heard a loud crash in the farmyard. Several dog-like creatures were trying to climb into a large shiny dustbin. They snapped and snarled at each other as they ate the farm scraps.

'Ere, watch it! Leave off! That bit's mine! Find your own dinner. Grrr!' This came from a large handsome animal with a red-brown coat. He had a bushy tail with a white tip, and he liked to show his teeth.

'Don't shout at her, you big bully, or I'll bite you! Grrr!' said another of the animals. Then there was a bit of rough and tumble:

'Mmm!'

'Ow!'

'Pack it in!'

'Get 'im off!'

'That hurt!'

'Grrr!' Several of the animals were fighting over a bone.

Several dog-like creatures were trying to
climb into a large shiny dustbin.

Esmeralda hung from a loose brick on the farm wall just above their heads, and watched them as they squabbled.

'What a noisy lot of feeders,' she thought. 'I don't think I'd like to eat that smelly mess. Excuse me,' she continued in a louder voice when there was a lull in the fighting, 'what are your names? Why do you eat rubbish?'

'Who said that?' said the handsome one, who seemed to be the boss. Raising his head, he saw Esmeralda and his eyes glinted. 'Grr, nosy, aren't you?' he growled. 'We're foxes, if you must know, and we live over there,' pointing his nose in the direction of Bluebell Wood. 'Are you nice to eat?'

'Oh dear, no,' squeaked Esmeralda, hastily spreading her wings and escaping into the night sky. She smelt the dog fox's stale breath as he leaped to snatch her. His teeth clashed, but he caught only empty air. Then, as she looked down, she saw that he had already forgotten her and was snapping at another fox's heels.

'What very nasty animals,' she grumbled to herself, 'and that one's really horrid! Fancy asking if I was good to eat!'

Many other birds and animals visited the farm. In late summer the sky was filled with the twittering of sharp-winged birds with red throats, who made their mud homes under the eaves of the house. They were still feeding greedily in the evening when the bats came out, but there were so many insects about that no one went hungry. They were the swallows and martins. Misty told Esmeralda that he had heard how they flew south before winter, crossing the great oceans to the warm shores of Africa. But they would not stay in one place long enough to answer Esmeralda's questions.

Down in the farmyard, she discovered that Peta and Louis were leaving out saucers of milk. One evening, swooping down, she saw something prickly sitting in the saucer making slurping noises. Its feet were in the milk and so was most of its long snout, and it was the strangest little mound of an animal she had ever seen. 'Hello there,' she called.

The animal stepped so smartly off the saucer that it upset most of the milk. It curled itself into a ball.

'Stupid, stupid!' Esmeralda heard it grumbling to itself. 'Caught out again. Not paying attention as usual. Badgers come – eat you up! Whose fault's that?' All this was muffled by the animal's fur and prickles.

'It's all right, don't be scared,' said Esmeralda. 'I'm not a badger. It's me, Esmeralda.'

A sharp snout and one beady eye peeped from the centre of the prickles. 'Who's Esmeralda?' asked the animal, and quickly curled up tight again.

'I'm a bat, and you're perfectly safe, I'm sure. Please unroll and talk to me.'

This time two beady eyes appeared. The animal looked at Esmeralda, who was stretched out on the rim of the water trough. Deciding that she was telling the truth, it unrolled. 'What a nerve, what a cheek!' it said angrily. 'Look at the milk! What's it to you who I am? I'm busy!'

'I'm sorry,' said Esmeralda, 'I really am. Won't you at least tell me your name?'

'Too cold for wandering about. No insects!'
shouted Mr Otchi Wichi.

'Mr Otchi Wichi,' said the animal in the same angry tone.

'Mr Ouchy whatsy?' As soon as she said it, Esmeralda knew she had made a mistake.

'Otchi Wichi! Don't be rude. Hedgehog to you. Wasting my time. Busy trying to eat. Got to get fat.'

'What for, Mr Otchi Wichi?'

'Questions, questions! Going to sleep for the winter,' said Otchi Wichi. 'Aren't you?'

'Oh,' squeaked Esmeralda. 'Is that what we do? I wondered why my tummy kept rumbling. I thought I was just being greedy.'

'Lots of us animals, 'specially us that comes out at night, sleep through winter. Too cold for wandering about. No insects!' shouted Mr Otchi Wichi. 'You'll learn. If you're clever!'

And with that he rudely turned his back on her and went snuffling away through the dark. Esmeralda, realising that her stomach was rumbling again, flew up to join her friends.

Soon Esmeralda and the other bats will leave the barn
and fly across the countryside to the high church tower.

Soon Esmeralda and the other bats will leave Farmer Hayden's barn as they do every winter, and fly across the countryside to the high church tower in the village of Barrowdown. Not even the striking of the bells will wake them, because they will have settled down to sleep the winter through. Then, in the spring when they wake up, Esmeralda will be ready to begin the next chapter of her life as a Pipistrelle bat.

# Nature Notes

You are most likely to see the Pipistrelle or common bat on a warm evening when it is patrolling at the edge of a wood or along a hedgerow. It flies silently, in quick darting bursts, snapping up gnats and other small flying insects.

Like all bats, the Pipistrelle is guided by its own radar system, which enables it to avoid bumping into objects even when the light is very poor.

Bats are mammals which are specially adapted for flight. Unlike birds, their wings are a leathery membrane which stretches between their long slender fingers. On their hind feet they have claws which allow them to get a grip on the rough surfaces of their chosen roosting place.

In the past, many foolish stories have been told about bats. They are, in fact, delightful animals to watch and to study.

# Activities

This story teaches us many things — so much that it is difficult to know where to start! Esmeralda experiences many things on her adventures and is helped by many people along the way. From the owls to Farmer Hayden, all give Esmeralda help, advice and love. Just like God with us! Read Matthew 7:7-12. Here, Jesus tells us that when we need help all we have to do is ask. Now that you have read this passage here are some questions to think about:

1. In the first part of the story, Esmeralda's mother tells her to return home before daylight. Why does she do this?

2. God has also given us rules to live by so that we may be happy. Can you think of some of these?

3. Later in the story, Esmeralda is helped by the owls and then Farmer Hayden. Jesus told a story called the Good Samaritan about one man who helps another. It

can be found in Luke 10:25-37. Think of times when people have helped you.

4.  Write a prayer thanking God for all these people. Ask him to help you help others.

*Other Activities*

1.  Draw a night picture with a moon, trees in silhouette and lots of bats in flight against the night sky.

2.  The word to describe an animal that, like a bat, comes out at night is 'nocturnal'. Try and think of as many nocturnal animals as you can. (Some are mentioned in this story!)